MOMMY
DO
MY
HAIR

By Yesenia Hernandez

Illustrated by LeVar J. Reese
Colorized by Lizzie Young

Editor: Jessica Carelock

ISBN: 978-1-943258-67-3

Published by Warren Publishing
Charlotte, NC
www.warrenpublishing.net
Printed in the United States

Mommy do my hair,
I promise to sit in the chair.

Mommy do my hair,
make it pretty with
some flare.

Mommy do my hair,
add the beads I like to wear.

Mommy do my hair,
let my afro blow in the air.

Mommy do my hair,
don't forget to mist
before you twist.

Mommy do my hair,
but stretch it out so
I don't say ouch!

Mommy do my hair,
put it down, I will not pout.

Mommy do my hair,
pull it up and leave
the top out.

Mommy do my hair
like my cousins,
the big girls.

Mommy do my hair,
give me a ponytail with curls.

Mommy do my hair,
take your finger
and make whirls.

Mommy do my hair,
I'll wear a headband
with pearls.

Mommy do my hair,
I would like to
have cornrows.

Mommy do my hair, put it up for my dance solo.

Mommy do my hair
divided in two big puffs.

Mommy do my hair,
make it big and full of fluff.

Mommy do my hair, across my face with straight bangs.

Mommy do my hair, I
would like for it to hang.

Mommy do my hair straight like my friend Kate's.

Mommy do my hair so
we can play patty cake.

Mommy do my hair just one more time, so I can go to sleep and wake up feeling fine.

Thank you for all you do, Mommy.
You're the best!

Now you can go to bed and get some rest.

CPSIA information can be obtained
at www.ICGtesting.com
Printed in the USA
LVHW07*0408230318
570854LV00004B/6/P